HARD LOAN

First published 1989
by Walker Books Ltd
87 Vauxhall Walk
London SE11 5HJ

©1989 Shirley Hughes

First printed 1989
Printed and bound in Italy by L.E.G.O., Vicenza

British Library Cataloguing in Publication Data
Hughes, Shirley
The big concrete lorry.
1. Picture books — Texts
I. Title
741
ISBN 0-7445-1137-2

A Tale of Trotter Street

The Big
Concrete Lorry

Shirley Hughes

WALKER BOOKS
LONDON

The Patterson family lived at number twenty-six Trotter Street. There was Mum, Dad, Josie, Harvey and little Pete. Also Murdoch, their dog.

Their house had a patch of garden at the back with a flower-bed, a washing line and an apple tree. In front there was only just room between the house and the street for some flower-pots and a couple of dustbins.

Josie had a room of her own. It was jam-packed with *her* things.

Harvey and little Pete shared the back bedroom. It was jam-packed with *their* things.

Murdoch had a basket in the kitchen. But often (though he wasn't supposed to) he slept at the bottom of Harvey's bed. Murdoch was a roly-poly dog who fitted nicely under Harvey's feet, like a plump hot-water bottle.

The Pattersons' hall was full of coats, boots, skate-boards
and buggies. The family living room was very often full of
Pattersons. Sometimes – when Josie was doing her homework
at one end of the table and Mum was cutting out a blouse at

the other end, and Dad was eating his supper in front of the television, and little Pete was playing with his toy cars, and Harvey and Murdoch were flopping about all over the sofa – it seemed as though the room was so full it would burst!

"We must have more space!" moaned Mum.

"We could move to a bigger house," said Dad, "if only big houses weren't so expensive."

All the family said that they couldn't possibly move to a new house. They loved Trotter Street far too much.

Then Dad had a good idea. "We could build an extension!" he cried.

Harvey wanted to know what an extension was. Dad explained that it was an extra room at the back, just like the one which Mr Lal had built next door. Mr Lal's extension was full of beautiful pot-plants and ornaments.

All the Pattersons thought that to have an extension like Mr Lal's would be a very good idea. So Dad brought home some brochures showing pictures of splendid extensions with happy people looking out of them.

"I'll put it up myself!" said Dad.

"Are you sure you can manage it?" Mum asked anxiously.

Dad said that Mr Lal and his son Rhajit, and Frankie and
Mae's dad from up the street, had promised to help him,
so it would be all right.

Next week, a delivery van drew up outside the Pattersons'
house and some men unloaded bits of wood and windows
and doors and stacked them in the back garden. This was
the extension, all in pieces.

"Now we need some bricks," said Dad.

A few days later another truck arrived. It had "JIFFY BUILDING CO" written on it and, underneath, "Joe and Jimmy Best".

"Load of bricks you ordered!" said jolly Joe Best, jumping down from the cab. Then he and Jimmy lowered the flap at the back of the truck and began unloading the bricks. They took them through the house and stacked them in the garden.

After they had driven off, Harvey, Josie and little Pete had a great time playing on the bricks, while Mum vacuumed away the dirty footprints left by Joe and Jimmy.

The following morning, Dad got up very early and put on his old trousers, saying that he was going to dig a foundation. Of course, Harvey wanted to know what a foundation was. Dad explained that it was a solid base for the extension walls to stand on.

Mr Lal came round after breakfast and helped Dad measure the space for the extension. They marked it out carefully with string, pegged to the ground. Then Dad, Mr Lal and Rhajit, and Frankie and Mae's dad began to dig a trench following the line of the string.

Little Pete thought all this was very interesting. He fetched his spade and began to dig too. So did Murdoch.

When the trench was finished, the men cleared the space where the floor was to be, put down bits of brick and rubble and covered them with a plastic sheet. Now everything was ready for the concrete. But first, an Inspector came to look at it, to make sure it had all been done properly.

Meanwhile, Josie and Harvey pretended that the extension was already built and they were having lunch inside. Josie imagined that it had pink wallpaper and Harvey imagined that there were curtains with a pattern of aeroplanes.

Dad was so tired the next day that he didn't get up early.
Mum took him a cup of tea in bed. While the rest of the family
were having breakfast, they heard a great noise in the street.

They all hurried outside. A lorry had arrived at their house.
It was huge! It had a big drum that turned slowly round and round
– CRRURK, CRRURK, CRRURK! On the side of the lorry was written
"JIFFY READY-MIX CONCRETE CO".

Out jumped jolly Joe Best.

"Load of concrete you ordered!" he called cheerfully.

"Not this morning, surely?" said Mum. "I'm sure we didn't…"

But it was too late. Jimmy had already pulled a lever and the big drum poured out a load of concrete, all in a rush. Slop! Slurp! Dollop! Splosh! Just like that! It landed in a shivering heap right outside the Pattersons' front door.

Dad rushed downstairs, pulling
on his trousers over his pyjamas.
"We weren't expecting you
today!" he shouted.

"That's OK. Just sign here," said
Joe. Then he leapt back into
his seat.

"It's quick-setting!" he called from the cab window.
"Be hard as a rock in a couple of hours. Better get busy!"

"But we haven't…" Dad called back.

But Jimmy was already revving up the engine. The big concrete
lorry roared away up the street in a cloud of dust.

"Quick!" cried Dad,
picking up a shovel.

"Quick!" shrieked Mum,
searching for a spade.

"Grab those buckets!"
"Fetch the wheelbarrow!"
"Run for the neighbours!"

"The quick-setting concrete is soon going to set!"
Never had the Pattersons moved so fast. Mum began to
shovel up the concrete into the wheelbarrow and trundle
it through the house, while Dad shovelled and smoothed
it down over the foundation at the back.

Josie and Harvey ran
to fetch Mr Lal and
Rhajit from next door,

and Frankie and Mae's
dad from up the street.

And they all came running.

The neighbours pitched in and shovelled and spread too.
Josie, Harvey and little Pete ran up and down with buckets.
Murdoch joined in, barking loudly.

Everyone laboured and struggled and fell over one another's
feet. They shovelled and heaved and trundled concrete from
the front of the house to the back. And steadily the heap on
the pavement grew smaller and smaller.

"Quick! It's beginning to set!" shouted Mum.

Everybody worked faster and faster.

"Done at last!" gasped Dad, throwing down his shovel and wiping his hands on his trousers.

Then all the workers rested. The foundation was finished. Only a small hill of concrete was left beside the front door. It had set so hard that nothing in the world would shift it.

The extension went up bit by bit. First, a low brick wall,
then the roof, windows and door.
And at last the Patterson family were able to move in.

They were so pleased with their beautiful new extension
that they gave a party for all their neighbours.

Harvey and little Pete were extra pleased with the small concrete hill which stood outside their front door. None of their friends had one like it. It was great for sitting on and for racing toy cars down.

And if you climbed up and stood on the top, you could see right to the very end of Trotter Street!